WELL READ!

GOOD WORK!

LET'S READ AGAIN!

I TRIED HARD!

HELP A FRIEND!

READING'S FUN!

LET'S READ AGAIN!

GOOD! WORD PERFECT!

LET'S TRY AGAIN!

BRILLIANT!

BE HELPFUL !

WELL DONE!

GOOD TRY!

WELL READ!

GOOD WORK!

EXCELLENT

WELL READ!

HONKING HORNS!

WELL READ!

TRY NEW THINGS!

LET'S HAVE FUN!

TAKE YOUR TIME!

TRY YOUR BEST!

GREAT WORK!

IT'S GOOD TO SHARE

GOOD EFFORT!

WORD PERFECT!

GREAT READING!

© Ludorum plc 2009

First published by Parragon in 2009

Parragon
Queen Street House
4 Queen Street
Bath BA1 1HE, UK

www.chuggington.com

© Ludorum plc 2009

ISBN 978-1-4075-6042-7

Printed in China

CAN'T CATCH KOKO

Based on the episode "Can't Catch Koko,"
written by Di Redmond and Sarah Ball.

Bath · New York · Singapore · Hong Kong · Cologne · Delhi · Melbourne

One sunny morning, Chuggington's fastest train, Harrison, was in the repair shed. He had broken down the night before and needed a new part.

CLANK!
CLANK!
CLANK!

"I need to be fixed fast, Morgan, or I won't be able to make the delivery run tonight," Harrison told the mechanic.

Koko **ZOOMED** excitedly into the fuel yard. She couldn't wait to tell Wilson and Brewster about Harrison. "Who's gonna do the night run if Morgan can't fix him in time?" asked Brewster.

It would have to be someone really fast...
Suddenly, Koko's eyes lit up. She could do it!

Koko sped into the depot and backed up next to Dunbar. "Oooh, please let me go, Dunbar," she begged. "I bet I can do the fastest run ever."

Koko had never done a night run before and Dunbar thought it would be a good experience.

"Traintastic!" cried Koko, excitedly. If only Wilson and Brewster weren't going too. Brewster was such a slow coach!

WOO WOO!

In a flash, the three
chuggers were loaded up with goods
and were ready to **RIDE THE RAILS!**

But as soon as the tunnel light appeared, Koko shot off ahead of Wilson and Brewster. "Bet you can't catch Koko!" she shouted, eager to make a speedy delivery.

At the other end of the tunnel, Wilson and Brewster caught up with Koko. The three friends gasped when they saw the beautiful, moonlit countryside around them.

TWIT-A WOO!

Wilson shuddered at the sound of the owl, but Koko whizzed on ahead.

"Betcha can't catch Koko!" she shouted.

Brewster and Wilson chugged after her. They had to stay together!

TWIT-A WOO!
TWIT-A WOO!

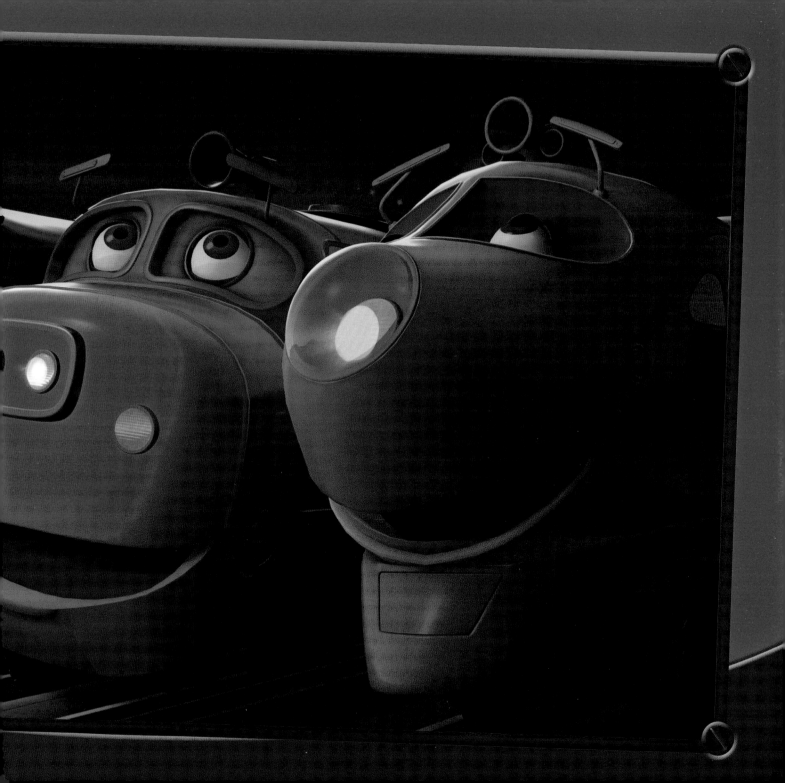

Koko rode down a side track and waited for Wilson and Brewster to appear.

ZOOOOOOOOOOOOOOO

CHUGGA, CHUGGA! CHOO, CHOO!

Koko could hear their engines getting closer.

A few moments later, Koko jumped out on them.

"BOOOO!"

she yelled, from the hidden track.

"You shouldn't do that Koko, I nearly fell off the track!" Brewster said, crossly.

"If you weren't so slow you would've seen me. ♪ ♪

BREWSTER'S A SLOW COACH!"

♪ Koko teased in a sing song voice.

But the chuggers didn't have time to mess around if they wanted to make the delivery on time. Koko raced off again, eager to impress Dunbar.

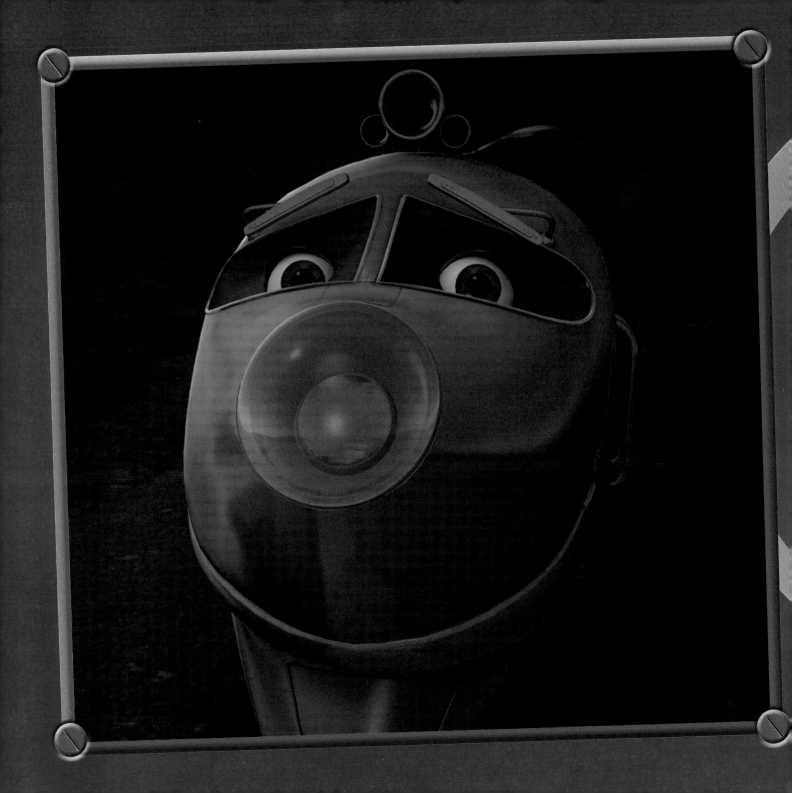

But then...

CREAK, CLUNK, SPLUTTER!

Koko's engine started to make a
funny noise and she stopped moving.

"Wilson? Come back – don't leave
me!" she pleaded.

But her friends had chugged
ahead and were too far
away to hear her.

Wilson and Brewster realised Koko was nowhere in sight. There were no lights on anywhere too – there must have been a power cut.

"Phew! Good job we're not electric then," said Brewster, feeling relieved. Wilson and Brewster both gasped – but Koko *was* electric...

Meanwhile, Koko was feeling sad and lonely. Just then, she heard something in the distance...

CHUG, CHUG, CHUG, CHUG...

It was Wilson and Brewster — they'd come back! Koko learned there was no power in the tracks to charge her engine. Now *she* was the slowcoach.

"I'm sorry I teased you, Brewster," she said quietly.

At the depot, Dunbar was worrying about the trainees.

Wilson suddenly came into sight, towing Koko behind him.

"WOOOOOOO OOOOOOH WOOOOOO OOOOOH!"

cried Wilson, making a loud siren noise.

"Breakdown chugger coming through!"

"Brewster's doing the night run all on his own," Koko told Dunbar.

At last, the power was back and Koko
whizzed up and down the track excitedly.

Vee's voice rang out.

I'VE JUST HAD A MESSAGE AND YOU'LL BE PLEASED TO KNOW THAT BREWSTER'S DELIVERED EVERYTHING ON SCHEDULE.

"What a hero! Wahay!" cried Wilson and Koko, proud of their friend. And Koko promised to never EVER call Brewster a slow coach again!

Visit VIRTUAL CHUGGINGTON

www.chuggington.com

Now you can ride the rails with Wilson, Koko and Brewster!

Honk your horns! Here in Chuggington we need more little engines to join us and keep things ship-shape. That means you, trainee!

- Paint your own engine
- Meet the chuggers
- Finish training tasks
- Play games
- Earn badges

Attention grown-ups!

Virtual Chuggington is a digital world where children can experience life from the same perspective as the engines. Think of it as a digital train set, one with enhanced play pattern and storytelling capability that will awaken your child's sense of wonder.

Join us here, won't you? We can't wait to learn, work and play together!

www.chuggington.com